Secrets & Lies
Volume 1

H.M. Ward

H.M. WARD PRESS
www.SexyAwesomeBooks.com

COPYRIGHT

This book is a work of fiction. Names, characters, places, and incidents are either the product of the author's imagination or are used fictitiously, and any resemblance to actual persons, living or dead, events, or locales is entirely coincidental.

Copyright © 2014 H.M. Ward
All rights reserved.

No part of this book may be reproduced, scanned, or distributed in any printed or electronic form.

H.M. WARD PRESS
First Edition: June 2014
ISBN-13: 9781630350307

CHAPTER 1

Is he serious? What an assface! I stumble through the quad, accidentally bumping shoulders with someone.

"Watch it, bitch." I look up to see a pointy-nosed girl surrounded by a pack of nasty friends, all sneering at me. I have no friends here, not yet.

The truth is, my life sucks. It's sucktacularly fucked up and I refuse to cry on the first day of college, but I'm having trouble swallowing the plate of shit my wonderful boyfriend just force-fed me. Excuse me, force-texted me. The asswipe texted me. He didn't even call. The more I think about it, the more my throat tightens. Breathing is overrated.

I mumble, "Sorry," and get the hell out of there, before they hogtie my ass and toss me down a flight of stairs. Not that I've ever seen anyone hogtied, but this is Texas, right? I'm out of my element, by far.

As I hurry away, I hear my roommate's voice ring out, "That's right, Bacon! You better run!" The girls all giggle like Chelsey just said the funniest thing they've ever heard. Great. She's leader of the bitch pack. Why can't I ever attract a psycho sans backup? My luck sucks. Have I said that? Well, bad luck is my key feature and the bane of my existence.

As I haul ass across the quad, my phone chirps. *Don't look at the screen. Don't look at it!* I chant to myself, but I can't. I have to see what he said. It might be an apology. He might be breaking up with his other girlfriend and texted me by accident. Uh, wait. That'd be worse. I think.

The thing is, we've been together since we were kids. Our parents used to joke that we'd be married one day, as if it were meant to be. It even felt like fate brought us together. On the day we met, I was playing outside when a terrified bunny chased Matt the two blocks from his house to my front yard. Running blindly, Matt mowed me down, leaving me for the bunny to attack instead of him.

Okay, this bunny was the size of a small dog and had a hunger for marigolds. In an effort to save their gardens from becoming rabbit food, the sweet little old ladies in the neighborhood were actively trying to poison it. I saved that rabbit from the wrath of the grannies and my prize was Matt. He called me cool names like Rabbit Slayer. Okay, it sounded cool in grade school, and much better than the normal nicknames kids give each other. Boogerface or Rabbit Slayer? Please. Like that's even a choice.

Matt and I have been together so long, I've forgotten what it feels like to be apart. Now the unthinkable has happened and I'm two thousand miles from home, completely on my own. Matt is everything to me.

I pluck the phone from my pocket and scan the screen.

There's this other thing…

Fuck. Like it could get worse. He already broke up with me. What's worse than that?

I type back, *I doubt it.*

No, you need to know. There's someone else. I'm in love with her, Kerry.

The prickling sensation hits the back of my eyes hard and fast. As I push through the door, I turn right and search for a bathroom. I can't fake my way through this. I can't sit here and pretend that he didn't just rip my heart out. How can there be someone else? I was his and he was mine. We were a couple. I have his damned ring on my finger. We were going to give this long distance relationship thing a chance.

But Matt didn't give it a chance.

A sob escapes my throat and my vision blurs. I race down the hallway, feeling the stares of strangers following in my wake. I can't cry now. I'm trying so hard not to, but my heart won't listen. It's curling into a ball and shriveling inside my chest. Grief takes hold of me, but I'm not crying yet. I try to find a restroom, holding back the cascade of sorrow that's building behind my eyes.

Plowing through the door, I head straight for the mirrors. There are always sinks by mirrors. I slam my books down on the counter and clutch the edge of the sink. Big gasping sobs wrack my body as I bend over the sink and stare at the white basin. Just as my tears start to fall, I see something move in the mirror. I feel eyes on me and the hairs on the back of my neck stand on end. I hadn't noticed anyone—not that I could see with my eyes full of tears.

Glancing up, I look across the room and don't understand what I'm looking at. A guy is standing by the wall. He's tall and toned, with dark hair and of standard build. At least, that's what he looks like through tears. Why is he in the girl's room? My brain is broken. I stand there and gape, not realizing that he's holding his thingy in his hand and standing in front of a urinal.

A crooked smile lines his lips when he sees me staring. "I, uh, think you're turned around."

His voice doesn't reach me. My body is in the middle of a full-fledged freak out and there's a guy in the ladies room, peeing on the wall. What the hell kind of school is this? I keep blinking, but I can't wrap my brain around what I'm seeing.

I manage to squeak out, "What?"

The guy zips up and gives me that pity look—you know the one. It says thank God

I'm not you, in the nicest way possible. "You're in the men's room. The women's room is down the hall."

This can't be happening. Horrified, I lunge for my books, but he steps to the counter to pick them up at the same time. We collide and his firm body smacks into mine. I stutter something incoherent, finally getting a good look at his face. Holy hotness! I never look at other guys, but once in a while someone that is supermodel perfect catches my attention. When people like that cross your path, it's impossible to look away. His beauty is blinding, and even through tears I notice his sexy smirk, mildly amused blue eyes, and perfectly smooth skin.

Add in his hard body and holy crap. I smacked into the hottest man I've ever seen, stared at his package, and made an ass out of myself. I'm still upset, but so mortified at the same time, that I no longer think and adrenaline takes over. Heart pounding, I push off his firm chest and right myself. My mouth dangles open as I try to form words, but my balance sucks and my hip bumps the books. They topple off the counter and clatter to the floor, while the rest of my stuff slides into the sink for a swim. I can't be this catastrophe. I can't face this hot guy with raccoon eyes, unable to do anything but grunt at him like a baboon.

There aren't many ways to play off a disaster of these proportions. I decide to do the only respectable thing and run like hell. Before he can say anything else, I'm out the door and down the hall. And we're talking full out run, not that little sissy girl run. I mean full out, an axe murderer is going to chop me up, run.

I hear his voice behind me, calling me to come back. Thank God I didn't put my name in my books, yet. I have enough problems without shit like this happening. Horrified, I think about how freaking weird I had to look standing there, mascara running, just staring at his thingy. I stared. What the hell is wrong with me? Who does stuff like that?

I shove through the door at the end of the hall and fly down the stairwell. I'm outside and into the parking lot before I slow down. Rasping for air, I round the side of the building and double over, struggling to breathe. I stand for a second before sliding my back down the wall and pulling my knees to my chest. I bury my face and let the tears fall.

CHAPTER 2

"Hey?" The voice is coming from my left. I spot a Chinese Slipper out of the corner of my eye and a long blue skirt. "Are you all right?"

I don't glance up. "Yeah. I'm fine." I've been sitting on the side of the building for a while. I completely blew off my art class. Great first day. Even if I can make it to my dorm room, I can't cry there because the roommate from Hell might walk in.

Slipper Girl sits down next to me and gives a gentle laugh. "Dude, you're a really bad liar."

"I know." We both offer up a nervous laugh. I chance it and peek out at her. I know

I look terrible. My face is puffy and smeared with makeup. I'm pretty sure my jeans are covered in snot. It's one of those moments where you wish you had the power of invisibility, but I don't. And she sees me. I haven't made a single friend since I got here, so I feel weird actually talking to someone. I give her a weak half-smile.

She pulls her knees into her chest, and wraps her arms around her ankles. The little black slippers stick out from under her skirt. "So, I'm thinking we need emergency ice cream and maybe—a frying pan."

What? I sit up a little bit and look at her. Slipper Girl has a pretty face and light brown hair that flows like a silky curtain from the top of her head to her waist. It's really long. "What's the frying pan for?"

"To smack the guy who made you cry like that on your first day."

I sniffle and swipe my eyes with the back of my hand. "Oh, I thought we were going to make stir fry."

She smiles at me. "You can cook?" She reaches into her little woven purse and hands me a tissue.

"Not really. I'm pretty good at burning

things and making food that's easy to cook but tastes really gross. How about you?"

"Eh," she tilts her hand back and forth. "So-so, but I make some badass cookies. They're orgasmic. Seriously. I'm the cookie queen." She laughs and looks bashful, which makes me smile. "So, since cooking dinner sounds less than tasty, there's this great Chinese place near here. Are you hungry?" The girl tucks a lock of hair behind her ear and motions to a nearby parking lot. "My car is right over there. We could eat and be back before the next class begins. What do you say?"

"I look like a train wreck."

"Yeah, you don't know this about me, but I'm not taking no for an answer. Everyone tells me yes. To everything. I'm spoiled rotten." She grins and flashes all her teeth before standing. Holding out her hand, she says, "Come on. I won't bite and I have an emergency Guys-Suck pack in my car. It has cookies, Midol, concealer, a baseball cap, and a pack of condoms. We can make balloon animals. I make a mean giraffe."

Wiping my eyes with the back of my hand, I say, "You had me at orgasmic cookies."

She laughs and helps me up. "They are. You better be ready, otherwise you'll be blushing, I'll have to pretend it isn't awkward, and we won't be able to look at each other. That's pretty lame, right?"

"Yeah, I have enough people to avoid eye contact with right now, anyway." A small smile spreads across my face, and my cheeks suddenly burn.

"I sense a story, here. What happened? You have to tell me."

"Nothing," I hedge, but a smile tugs at my lips and a fresh blush burns under my cheeks.

"You can totally tell me! I won't say a word." I follow her to a new white Volvo parked at the back of the lot. She throws her bag in the back seat as I get in on the passenger side. "Oh, dude—my name is Beth. Beth means keeper of secrets." She shoots me a winning smile and starts the car.

"I'm Kerry."

"So, spill. What's your major and all that?" She starts the car and pulls out of the parking lot.

"I'm Kerry Hill, an art major from New

York. My boyfriend dumped me this morning via text message, and I was so upset that I mistakenly walked into the men's bathroom right before class. While there, I bumped into a super-hot guy, saw his, uh—package—and stared. After that, I made friends with the brick wall until you came along. It's a pretty pathetic first day of college."

Her jaw drops and she stares at me for way too long. Since we're in moving traffic, it's alarming. The girl is the worst driver I've ever seen. I'm having trouble not screaming. The light is yellow and about to flip to red and she's not slowing down. "You have me beat. Beth Gallub from Seattle, the youngest of four siblings, with three overprotective brothers that follow me everywhere. Ten bucks says one of them shows up before your class later. No joke."

"Awh, you're the baby."

"Psh. Yeah. It sucks monkeys, man. What about you? Do you have siblings?"

"Yeah, an older brother and a younger sister."

"So, you're the pathologically needy middle child."

"Psych major?"

She laughs. "How'd you know?"

"A hunch. You seem like the kind of person who can't pass a crying chick on the sidewalk." I laugh and the rest of my nerves flutter away. I relax as much as I can pretend to with Beth driving. Seriously. People in Seattle must not think lines are important. The girl is all over the road.

Finally, she pulls into the parking lot for the Chinese restaurant. We get out, head into the buffet and grab a table.

After we eat and talk about our horrible first days—mine takes the loser cake—Beth leans back in the booth and watches me. "So, it's rebound night, right?"

I shift in my seat and scrunch my face. "Not unless we're talking about a cake rebound."

Beth shakes her head. "The fastest way to get over a broken heart isn't a lifetime in a shrink's chair, it's screwing another guy. That severs the connection, so the next time you meet a guy you're really into you won't compare him to your ex. If you still feel an emotional connection to your ex, you'll compare sex with the new guy to sex with your ex—which will make you an emotional basket case." She pauses for a second, then leans forward, a curious expression on her face. "What do you usually do to get over a guy?"

This feels personal and the urge to make something up comes over me, but I don't do it. Instead, I tell her the lameball truth. "I haven't broken up like this before. We were together for a long time." My eyes drop to the table and my throat tightens, but there are no more tears. I won't cry for him again, but that doesn't ease the pain flowing from the center of my chest.

"Oh, that's rough." Beth glances over my shoulder and waves at someone. I don't turn, because it's just a passing gesture. She didn't wave the person over, but before I know it, there's a guy standing at the table. Beth rolls her eyes. "What did I tell you? This is my brother, Josh. One of them. This is Kerry. Note the boobs. She's a chick. Now, leave me alone."

My face turns bright red when she directs him to look at my chest, but he seems to be used to her antics. At least I hope that's it, because he doesn't look. Josh is a nice looking guy and faintly resembles Beth. He's on the shorter side, built with broad shoulders and gold-streaked brown hair. It's pulled back into a ponytail. "When you didn't show up, Justin asked me to check on you."

Beth groans and fake shoots herself in the head, before falling sideways into the booth, and then disappears under the table. "I have my own life," she whines from the bench.

"Obviously. You're very mature." Josh flashes a smile my way and slips into the booth next to me. I slide over and Beth sits up, a plastic smile on her face.

"I am," she says, smoothing her skirt and raising both her eyebrows excessively high. "Kerry and I were discussing rebound sex. Would you like to enlighten us with your wisdom regarding the best course of action following a break up?" She folds her hands on the tabletop and smiles like a deranged secretary.

Josh laughs once and looks over at me. "Was your relationship serious?"

"Very," Beth answers for me. "What's the best way to move on?"

He looks at me a moment longer than I expect him to. "I don't know you, Kerry, but the only way to get over anyone is to move on. Rebounding is one way, but—"

Beth cuts him off. "But it's not for the faint of heart. Oh my God. You're such a dick. There's no way in hell that I'm letting her hook up with you, assface, so drop it." For a second I think Beth is being too harsh. He wasn't going to hit on me, but then Josh laughs and relaxes.

He bumps his shoulder against mine. "Fine, but I had to try. She's hot." Glancing over at me he says, "Have sex with a stranger to cut the cords and wipe the slate clean. It's the fastest way out of the hellhole you're in right now. And I strongly suggest you pick the guy or some dickwad will play you."

"Like you?" Beth asks, sticking out her tongue at him. Josh smiles.

"Exactly like me, and since I know Beth, you'd have to see me again, which would suck. My advice—pick a guy from a bar on the other side of the city, making the odds of running into him again unlikely." He swipes Beth's glass and downs the rest of her soda.

"So, people really do this? No one will think I'm a slut? It seems kind of crazy to walk up to some guy and say, what? I need to get laid. Wanna have sex with me?" This conversation is making me really uncomfortable.

Josh laughs. "Well, don't say it like that. You sound crazy. You need to make him think you've done it before or you'll set off his psycho-bitch alert."

"Guys don't have that, Josh. And does it really matter what she says? No one listens after they hear 'do you want sex?'" Beth tilts her head to the side and makes a face, like she thinks guys are mindless zombie folk.

"You should tell him that you're not looking for a relationship and ask him if he wants to do something. Let him offer." Josh turns to me and studies the side of my face. "You've only been with one guy?"

I nod. "Yeah."

"Was he good? Ouch! Beth, what the hell?" He shifts next to me and clutches his leg under the table.

"You can't ask her that! I met her, like, an hour ago and you're already asking if her ex satisfied her sexually? God, Josh! Go to the store and buy some manners."

Josh cringes. "I didn't say it like that."

The two of them are like a comedy act. I

can tell they love each other, but they both have very different, chaffing personalities. "It's okay," I offer, and they stop squabbling and look at me. "I don't have a reference point outside of my ex—he was my first and only."

Beth looks horrified. "You thought you were going to be together forever, didn't you? Oh my God. Josh, don't be a dick, hug her."

I laugh nervously and scoot toward the wall, "Yeah, that's okay. I really don't—well, okay." Before I can get away, Josh throws his arms around me and squeezes hard, mashing my body against his in a bear of a side-hug. I choke, "I'm fine. Really."

"You poor kid!" He releases me and slips out. "Beth, I can head out there with you after seven. If you want to go before then, call Jace."

Beth's jaw tightens and she doesn't look at him. "You're not coming."

Josh smirks and chuckles. "You're funny." He kisses the top of her head and Beth mashes her lips together like she's going to explode. "See you ladies tonight. Oh, and Kerry—dress like you want a good time." He winks at me and rushes out.

CHAPTER 3

I get dressed in Beth's room out of fear my horrible roommate will figure out what's going on and ruin it for me. I've only been here a few days, but she's already turned half the dorm against me. Well, maybe that's an overstatement, but it feels like truth.

Beth pulls a red dress from her closet. The neckline is a deep V and the fabric is slinky. "Try this. It's my lucky dress. Guys will slobber all over you."

I take it and look for a place to change, but the room is a box. There's no privacy. Beth notices my hesitation and walks over to the closet. She pulls a door, leaving it halfway open. "Change behind here. How are you this old and still this shy?"

"I don't know. Nothing turned out the way I thought it would. That's all." I strip my tee shirt off and slip the dress over my head before stepping out of my jeans.

"You realize that having sex with a random guy tonight means he's going to see you naked, right? You can't act like a virgin or you'll freak him out." The bedsprings give and I know she's sitting down.

"What do you mean?"

"Uh, you can't hide behind doors and under sheets. You have to strut around like you own that sinfully curvy body. I wish I had hips. I'm assless. It makes me sad." Beth looks up when I step around the door. The dress is skintight. I tug at the fabric and try to pull the hemline down. If I bend over, my butt will peek out.

Beth jumps up and races over. "Holy shit. You look hot. Do you see this?" With a huge smile on her face, she pulls me in front of the mirror.

"I don't know. You don't think that it makes me look fat?"

Beth gives me a face that says she'd kill for my body, but it's hard to believe. She's cute and I feel bulky standing next to her. "You have it all—tits and ass with a tiny waist. Besides, sexiness is a state of mind. If you think you're sexy, you will be. It's confidence. Put on a fake persona tonight and toss your self-image issues out the window. We can blame your mother for ruining your life another time."

Beth styles my hair and applies my makeup. By the time she's done, I don't recognize myself. My hair falls in silky waves and my lips are dark red. I look like a model. I look like someone else. It feels really weird to look into a mirror and not recognize the image staring back. I want to back out, but I can't now. Beth is ready to go. She throws on a cute dress with a frilly skirt that comes to her knee.

"Why do you get to dress like that?" I'm practically whining.

Beth steps into her little black slippers and explains. "It's for comparison purposes. If I'm wearing a little church dress, you look like the slutty one. All the guys will look at you first and ignore me, which is what we want."

Once we're both ready, we head to her

car and make our way toward the other side of the city. For a second, I worry about what will happen when I actually get there, but Beth's driving distracts me. Suddenly, I'm taking way too many deep breaths and trying not to scream. As she careens down a ramp insanely fast, my reflexes overpower my desire to be polite and I grab hold of the oh-shit strap.

Beth apologizes. "I don't usually hit stuff. I promise." Somehow that doesn't make me feel better. I just nod. "Plus, this is a Volvo. You have my brothers to thank for that. They told my parents it was the safest car out there. They got cute little convertibles for graduation. I got a soccer mom car. Bastards. So what do you drive?"

"Nothing at the moment. I thought things would be within walking distance."

"Yeah, they're really not—unless twenty miles back and forth to the mall doesn't faze you. We'll have to go car shopping one day."

Sure, if I live that long. By the time we get to the bar, I'm a ball of nerves. My stomach churns and I feel sick. I'm standing next to the Volvo in the parking lot, waiting for Beth. "I can't do this." I'm ready to jump back in the car, but she locks the doors before I can yank mine open.

"Yes, you can. You want to get over your ex, right?" I nod. "Then you know what to do. Listen, I don't want to pressure you into anything. If you decide not to ask anyone, then don't. But we drove all the way here. Let's at least have a good time before we head back. Okay?"

I can do that. I can have a good time and laugh even though I wish I were at home, on my mom's couch, crying like a baby. No, it's fine. I can totally do this and Beth's right. Just because I go inside, doesn't mean I have to go through with it. I can chicken out.

Beth and I walk in and I instantly feel eyes on me. They travel over my body, overtly sizing me up. I won't be shy and timid. Not tonight. As Beth and I head toward a table, I notice a guy looking me over and suddenly I don't mind so much. Being desired feels good. We sit down at a table and order drinks. We sip and talk about nothing for a while. I'm not seeing the right guy and I don't want to have sex with someone that doesn't give me a good vibe. I don't want a pushy guy. Actually, I prefer shy guys and realize this whole '*wanna do me?'* thing might not work on a shyer man.

Josh tries to join us, but Beth shoos him away, so he takes up residence at another table that quickly fills with women. How did he do that? He smiles a lot and has this lazy body language that seems to act like girl-nip. They go crazy for it.

After two hours, I'm ready to call it quits. "There's no one here that's even close to my type."

Beth slurps the bottom of her daiquiri. "He doesn't have to be your type."

"Are you seriously advocating that I do it with an ug-o?"

Beth snorts and nearly chokes. "No! That's not what I meant."

"Good, otherwise I'd have to worry about you trying to pawn me off on one of the janitors in the dorm."

She grins wickedly. "That was my plan for tomorrow night."

"Loser," I tease and shake my head.

"I'm not the one who can't get laid," she laughs. It's weird how fast she feels like a friend. I kick her under the table. "Hey!"

"I can so get laid! I just want him to be…" my eyes drift across the room and I see him – Mr. Right. A guy is sitting alone at a back corner table, wearing a red ball cap. His face is downcast and there's a sketchpad in front of him. My voice dies in my throat as I stare. He's perfect.

Beth turns around in her seat. "Seriously?"

I pull my eyes off of him just as he looks up. "Why? What's wrong with him?"

"Nothing, if you like that serial killer vibe."

"He's an artist."

"Ten bucks says there's nothing drawn in that sketch pad."

I don't like her bashing my mystery man. "No, he's not using that as a ploy. He's real."

Beth is trying not to laugh. "You are so naïve."

"I am not." I say it dreamily as I watch him move the pencil across the paper, and then flip it over, smudging the page with the eraser.

"Okay, so let's make a bet. If he's a fake, I win and you have to buy me a piece of cake. If he's a real artist, then you win and you have to ask him. Deal?" I don't answer. Instead, I squirm in my seat and try not to look at him.

"What's the matter? If he's the artsy type, you found what you were looking for. If he isn't, I get cake. It's a good bet."

"She won't do it." Josh suddenly appears. He's standing next to Beth and smiles at me in that smug way that only truly spoiled men can pull off. "She doesn't have it in her."

"You're an asshole." My gaze flicks up and meets his, while Beth laughs.

"I know. I'm okay with it. But, you're a nice girl, and you'll stay that way. There's no way you can work up enough nerve to walk over there and ask that guy to sleep with you."

"Yeah, well watch me." Who said that? My pride is whooping and slapping me on my back.

Suddenly, I'm out of my seat and making a beeline toward Mystery Man. He's concentrating on his drawing and doesn't look up. I'm so nervous, I want to die. What if he shoots me down? What if he just laughs? I don't think I could bear it. Stop thinking! Just say it. Just say it. Don't wait for him to look up. Don't wait for him to have a chance to say anything. Just spit it out.

As soon as I'm by his table, I say, "Listen, I'm not looking for a relationship and you look a little bit lonely over here. Maybe we could go someplace and fix that?" My voice is confident and flows like warm honey. I'm so proud, I actually manage a sexy smile and slip into the booth opposite him.

When he looks up, I literally choke. "It's you!" Before I can recover, I sputter some ungodly sound and gape at him.

"So, is that what you were doing in the men's room this morning? The school really frowns on soliciting." The corners of his lips twitch, like he's trying not to laugh at my shock. Those sapphire eyes seem amused. He taps his pencil on the table and looks me over. "Although, when they put up the signs, I doubt they had that kind in mind."

My jaw hits the table, and I'm still frozen in place. Holy fuck, he's hot and that teasing tone doesn't help. My mind is screaming at me to run, but I can't move. Something about the moment has the mesmerizing quality of headlights, and I'm sitting like a deer waiting to be struck between the eyes.

Pull it together, Kerry! I shake off my shock and stand to leave, but he reaches out and grabs my wrist. I glance down at him, waiting to see what he's going to say.

"I didn't say no. I'm just making sure that I don't have a hooker stalking me."

Pressing my hand to my chest, I say sweetly, "How flattering, but no thanks. I've changed my mind." Tearing my wrist from his grip, I turn to sprint away, but he jumps up from his booth and follows me.

"Wait a second. Don't be like that. I was just kidding. Really." I stop and turn back to face him. Mistake. Those eyes are so blue and so sincere that I can't blow him off. A nervous tick appears in the corner of his mouth, making it twitch. "Can I show you something?"

"I've already seen it, thanks."

He laughs once, loudly, and gently takes my hand, pulling me back to his table. "You've got a sharp tongue when it's not tangled. Seriously, come here. I want to show you what I was sketching." He stops in front of the table and picks up the pad, flipping backwards through the pages.

I glance side to side and see Beth waving at me from across the room. It's such a dorky thing to do, but it makes me laugh. I swat at her and turn back to see what this guy is doing. "My friend thought the whole artsy thing was a ploy to pick up girls. We actually made a bet."

He looks intrigued. "Really? What were the terms?"

"If she wins, and you're a loser with an empty sketch pad, she gets cake."

"You bet that I wasn't a fake?" I smile, and slide my eyes to the side, nodding. "Interesting. So what do you get if you win?"

My face feels hot, but I say it anyway. "You." Tonight, I'm not me. I'm confident, sexual, and everything I'm totally lacking in real life.

Smiling shyly, he looks down and hands me the pad before sitting in the booth. "I'm afraid your friend lost her cake."

The smile slips off my lips when I see what he's drawn. It's me. My long smooth wavy hair is obscuring my face, but it's certainly me, my little nose, and this slutty dress. But the way he drew me sitting in the booth opposite Beth—I don't know—I look ethereal and unapproachable. He drew me as if I were just out of his reach.

I stare at it for a second before looking over at him. "I bet you drew every woman in here."

"I don't recall that being part of the bet, but go ahead and turn the page." He offers a crooked smile.

I flip through the pad and see saltshakers, lamps, the back of a waiter carrying too much food, and other things that are utterly ordinary. He captured the weight of the tray and the way it tips to the side slightly, like it might fall. Even the objects that he drew on the table seem evocative. When I look at him, he offers a weak smile and reaches for the pad. "I don't usually share this. It's like a journal."

I know what he means. I don't show my sketches to anyone. They reflect the state of my mind, and my heart. He's braver than I am, showing those things to a total stranger. For a moment, I don't know myself. I'm not me. Reaching out, I extend my hand and say it again, "I'm not looking for a relationship."

He takes it and stands. Looking into my eyes, he breathes, "Neither am I."

A smile spreads across my face as my heart pounds harder. "Then let's get out of here."

Nodding, he leads me toward the door. On the way out, I pass Beth's table and grin.

"You lost."

She gives me a huge grin. "Yeah, but you hit the jackpot."

I did, didn't I? He's hot, funny, shy, and artistic. He's my dream guy. For only one night, he can't be anything less.

CHAPTER 4

We drive to a hotel down the street and before I know it, we're tangled together in a dark little room, his lips on mine. My heart keeps telling me I'm cheating on Matt even though my brain reminds me that we're over. Since I'm not a cheater, I understand why Beth was telling me to do this. If I wanted something with this guy, he'd have to live up to Matt in every single way.

Gasping for air, he breaks the kiss and sits up a little bit. We're lying on the bed, side by side. Pushing up on an elbow, he looks down at me. "I never got a chance to ask your name. I'm—"

I press my fingers to his lips, "No names.

Say anything you like. We can do anything we want without worrying about tomorrow. There is no tomorrow for us." As I speak, I slip the shoulders of my dress off and the bodice crumples around my waist, revealing my bra. The black lace fabric is sheer, and I know he can see right through it. It took a long time for me to be comfortable being naked in front of Matt, but I don't have time to feel timid with this guy. My mystery man's eyes darken as I slip out of the dress and lay back on the bed. The matching panty covers my front but showcases the curves of my ass.

His eyes drink me in, but he hesitates. Something flashes across his face, but I can't tell what it is. Regret? I wonder what ghosts are plaguing him right now, and I wonder if they're as strong as the memories of Matt that keep wandering through my mind. I have to do this. I can't let Mystery Man back out, and it feels like that's what he's about to do, so I take things a step further. I sit up and unhook my bra. Reaching behind me, I pull it off and hold it between two fingers before dropping it to the floor, my eyes locked on his face as I do it. The lights are on, and this is so weird for me, but I do it anyway. I can't even fathom the person I would be if I didn't hate my body, if I didn't scold myself for every excess ounce of fat. I can't imagine a world without those checks to guide my decisions. I'd be someone else, and in the moment I am.

Mystery Man is sitting up, so I crawl over to him and swing my leg over his lap, straddling him. He sucks in air as I settle in place. My pulse is pounding in my ears and I try not to consider what he must think of me, what he must think of what I'm doing. I think he's beautiful. From the look in his eye, I know he wants me. His hands slip up my sides, feeling my ample curves, and then back down again. He cups my butt and pulls me to him, his lips crushing down on mine. The kiss grows hotter as our tongues tangle in my mouth. I spread my hands on his chest, tugging at his shirt, trying to get it off. We break apart long enough to pull the fabric over his head and then he presses his bare chest against me. I feel his warm skin and toned muscles slipping against my breasts.

Matt didn't have this guy's muscles. Each one is so perfectly defined that I want to lick him from head to toe. I trace my fingers over his arms, feeling the strength in them, while the pulsing between my thighs increases. He's hard beneath me, so when I start to rock my hips he moans into my mouth through our kiss. Breaking apart, I rise up and press my breasts to his face. Mystery Man wants me, but he's holding back. I can tell because when I do it, he stiffens and the hesitation is there again.

"Kiss me, baby." I moan the words and drag my nipples across his stubbled jaw. Before I get far, he reacts. His lips part and he takes me in his mouth, sucking my breast and flicking my nipple with his tongue. Oh, God, it feels good! Matt didn't do it like this. He'd either slobber on me or gnaw my nipple off.

But Mystery Man doesn't do that. He's slow and teasing, alternating between licking and sucking, teasing my nipple between his lips. His teeth graze my breast, making me speak words I normally couldn't say. I feel his smile as he pulls away and switches to the other side. Firm hands travel over my body, holding me against his mouth. As if I'd pull away? That'll never happen. I'm losing myself in him. Thoughts of Matt are scattering and I can't resist the longing between my thighs much longer.

As he kisses me, I reach down, undo the button on his jeans and lower the zipper. I want to free his hard length from the fabric. This man makes me feel like a goddess. His kisses are worthy of praise and his touch is so sensual. Lust fills my mind as I think about riding him and feeling him inside of me. He nips my nipple before pulling away. I move aside as he tugs at his jeans like he can't get them off fast enough.

He tosses the jeans to the floor and stands beside the bed, wearing just his boxers. He grins a wicked smile and motions toward me with his hand. "Ladies first." He tugs at his own waistband and I understand what he means. "I want to see you naked, spread out on the bed, begging me to fuck you."

The pit of my stomach drops when he talks like that and I'm surprised that I like it. Nervous anticipation floods through my body, but I do as he says. Shimmying out of my panties, I toss them aside and lie back on the bed and let him look.

Those blue eyes are so dark and sexy. His lips part the slightest amount as his eyes drift below my waist, taking in the smooth skin between my legs. He grins, like I'm some sort of siren because I had a Brazilian. "You are so sexy. I can't wait to have you."

"Then take me." I never say things like that, but I can't help it. He makes me feel good and I can't wait to come in his arms. It will cut Matt off, ending that part of my life.

Hot Guy loses his boxers and comes back to the bed. His body is beyond words and, when I see how much he wants me, the size of him, I tremble and grip the sheets. He crawls toward me, and kisses me, starting at my toes. He works his way up my legs, kissing the V once, before continuing up toward my mouth. He straddles me, pinning my thighs together, rubbing against me as he showers me with little kisses that drive me wild. I can't take it. I need him.

Clawing his back, I arch into him, and he dips his head to my breast, sucking and teasing me, taking me higher and higher. I'm losing it. I can't hold onto my mind and my thoughts drift away. I don't realize I'm talking until I hear my voice begging him to take me. "Please, baby, please." I tell him how much I want him inside me and so many other things I've never said to anyone.

His kisses drift to my neck, which makes

my flow of words increase. By the time he finally lets me splay my legs, I'm ready for him. I think he's going to push into me, but he drops to my chest, breathing hard and starts to kiss my stomach. Each kiss drops lower and lower, heading for the spot between my legs. I can barely hold myself together as I anticipate his mouth down there.

But then, everything shatters. The phone rings and he freezes. The noise is jarring, and another guy might have thrown the thing on the floor, but he doesn't.

Mystery Man pulls away from me and sits up. He reaches for the receiver and answers the phone. "Yes?" His voice is casual, like he wasn't doing anything important.

I'm horrified. What the hell? He doesn't look back at me or apologize. I roll to my side and pull the sheet up around me. Maybe it's nothing. Maybe he's not blowing me off. Hot Guy dips his head and releases a long slow breath as he runs his fingers through his hair. "I see. Thank you for calling." He hangs up and sits there, still for a second. I watch his back expand as he breathes, but he doesn't look at me.

Without explanation, he stands, and pulls

on his clothes. "I need to go. Please, call a cab." He pulls out his wallet and drops a fifty on the dresser, then turns on his heel. He's through the door before I have a chance to answer.

CHAPTER 5

"So, how was he?" Beth has a stack of pancakes covered in syrup. She's intently decorating them with Fruit Loops, one at a time, as if it were a Christmas tree.

I didn't tell her last night. It was too embarrassing. I stumbled into my bed and fell asleep. It's seven in the morning and I feel like I've been hit by a truck, physically and emotionally, because getting rejected by the rebound guy was the most god-awful thing that could have happened.

"Great," I answer, not offering more details. He was great—right up until he ran back to his girlfriend or whoever called and busted us up. Maybe he's a loser and I should be glad we didn't do it, but the thought doesn't help. Not knowing why he ran off makes me think I did something wrong. It doesn't make sense, not with the phone call. Who answers the phone during sex anyway? I want to slam my head into the table, but I don't. I smile at Beth and shove a spoonful of eggs into my mouth.

"Great sounds like an understatement. That guy was your dream man." She starts shoving her sugary breakfast into her mouth. We're sitting in the middle of the cafeteria with the rest of the people who eat breakfast. There's hardly anyone here.

"Yeah, he was." She gives me a look that says she knows something is up. My shoulders slump as I lean my head on my hand and sigh. "Fine, I'll tell you the truth. He ditched me."

Beth spews the forkful of food. "He did what?" She looks as shocked as I felt. Her big blue eyes are dinner plates.

I poke at my eggs. "We were about to, you know, and then the phone rang. He answered it, tossed me money for a cab, and left."

Beth clutches the table, as if she's planning on tossing it into the wall. "Oh, my

God! What a jackass. Are you okay? You know it wasn't you, right? What kind of asshole answers the phone during sex?" Beth looks indignant. She releases her death grip on Mr. Table and waves at someone behind me without altering her mood or hiding her disgust. A second later a clone of Josh is sitting next to me. "Hey, Jace, complete this sentence: A guy who answers the phone during sex is…"

Jace laughs, and says, "Not into it." Beth kicks him under the table. "Hey! Keep your pointy witch shoes to yourself," he yelps.

Beth looks horrified and says to me. "That is not what it means! Kerry was with a guy last night and he knew it was a one-nighter, strictly rebound sex. But, while they were doing it, he answered the phone and left."

"Don't tell your brother that! God, Beth." I bury my face in my hands to hide my horror.

Jace looks me over. I feel his eyes slip up and down my body, before he answers. "So, a one-nighter, with her," he jabs his thumb my way, "and this guy answers the phone and leaves?"

"Yeah. Asshole, right?" Beth asks.

Jace talks to the side of my face, because I don't take my hands down. "You want the truth or the sugar coated version?"

I look over at him. "The truth, please. It can't be worse than what I already think."

He nods. "When did he leave? Like, what were you doing?"

My cheeks burn as my eyes drop to the table. "Yeah, he was doing me. Or about to…" Holy frack, this is the weirdest conversation I've ever had. I want to crawl under the table and die.

"Like things were all hot and heavy, he's about to nail you, but he answers the phone instead?" His dark brows inch together. I nod and then Jace's hand lands gently on my shoulder. "That guy wasn't worth your time."

"I said no sugar coating, Jace. Just tell me."

His hand falls down to the table before he leans in closer and says in a low voice, "He was using you to kill time. Maybe a cheater, maybe not. Either way, that phone call was more important than you were or he wouldn't have left."

"Jace!" Beth throws syrup-covered cereal

at her brother. "I wanted you to make her feel better, not worse!"

He swats them away, but one manages to stick to his shirt. He plucks it from the fabric and pops it in his mouth. "The truth hurts, little sister. It's better that she learns it now. If you see that guy again, don't waste your time on him." Jace gives me a sympathetic look and leaves our table.

CHAPTER 6

The rest of the day passes with no embarrassing incidents. I even manage to be in the art building without bumping into the bathroom guy. I was worried he went to school here, but he's not around. Maybe it was a fluke. Thank God.

I choose a stool toward the back of my figure drawing class. A sloppily dressed guy wearing clothing three times his actual size takes the seat next to me. His jet-black hair hangs down, obscuring his face. He sighs, like he wishes he were somewhere else, then glances over at me. "Hey, I'm Carter."

"Kerry. Are you an art major?" I haven't seen him before, but then again I don't have many upper level classes. When the department chair reviewed my portfolio, he let me skip ahead into a few advanced classes.

He smirks. "You're a freshman. How'd you get in here? This is a junior level class."

I shrug. "They thought I could handle it."

He points at my sketchbook and says, "May I?"

It's personal and I don't show it to people, but I have a feeling that I'm going to be stuck next to this guy all semester and if he doesn't think I should be here, well, things won't go very well. I hand it over and stare straight ahead. I don't suck. A New York City art school, one of the best in the world, offered me a full ride—all fees paid—if I enrolled there. So sitting in Drawing III isn't really anything major.

Carter flips through slowly, his dark eyes scanning my work. The corners of his mouth twitch like he's trying not to smile. He hands it back to me. "Not bad, freshman."

"Well?" I say and reach out my hand.

"Well, what?"

"Nice try, Carter, but you know how this works. I only show you mine if you show me yours. Flash me. Dazzle me with your—" as

I'm talking, he rolls his eyes and forks over the sketch book. When I flip it open, I can't speak. My jaw drops when I see what he's drawn. I forget that he's watching me out of the corner of his eye for a second and just stare. My fingers are drawn like magnets to the page. It's a drawing of him—Mystery Man.

I want to slip my fingers over his face and feel the life-like stubble under my fingertips. The drawing captures his somber mood perfectly. There's a lostness in his eyes that's impossible to hide. I saw it the other day when I slammed into him in the bathroom and then again at the hotel room. My heart flutters and I can't hide the emotions that are coursing through my body. But embarrassment still lingers, fresh in my mind. Who walks out in the middle of sex?

I flip the page and study detailed drawings of old benches with splintering wood beams, broken fences, and page after page of beautifully captured destruction and deterioration. Carter breathes life into his drawings. They don't just look like things. They look like they live and breathe. They look like they could jump off the page.

Though the inanimate objects look as if they live and breathe, the only drawing of an actual living, breathing person in the entire sketchbook is that first one. For a split second I worry that he's a friend of Bathroom Boy, or worse—that they're roommates.

I force a smile that I hope looks normal. To me, it feels like a robot is pulling on my cheeks, forcing my lips to curve. "Impressive," I say as I hand the pad back to him.

Carter lifts a dark brow at me. "Some people say that about him. You seem a little infatuated there, Kerry."

"I am not." Oh shit. I shouldn't have said that. I glance at Carter, but he just laughs.

"It's okay. A lot of people act like that, all star-struck and shit. It's hysterical."

A deep throaty *nah-ah* laugh comes from somewhere inside my chest. "I am not some lovesick idiot. I thought it was an amazing drawing, that's all. You've got mad skills. Learn to take a compliment, Carter." I glance at him out of the corner of my eye and tuck my hair behind my ear.

Carter grins at me, folding his arms over his chest and slumps back in his seat. "Yeah, that explains it."

Before I have a chance to reply, the professor walks in. Since I missed the first day, I have no idea what we're doing. An awful sinking feeling creeps up my throat. I feel like I'm going to vomit until Carter hands me his syllabus. I mouth thank you, and look it over.

The teacher is an old guy that looks an awful lot like the sculpture professor. Maybe they're brothers or something. He has snowy hair and a neatly trimmed white beard that covers his face. When he speaks, his bright green eyes sparkle like he's still a young man.

"The critique process that you've done with other professors is moot. In this class, you will study the drawing, say one thing that you like and say one thing that would make it better. That's it. We'll start at this end of the room and work our way around to, uh…" he glances at the seating chart, and then back up at me, "to Carter and, I'm sorry, but who are you? You're not listed here."

Every set of eyes turns my way. I hate it when that happens. Swallowing hard, I say, "I'm Kerry Hill. I missed the first class. I'm probably not on your seating chart yet."

The old man suddenly hates me. He cocks his head to the side and glances around the room. After a moment, he spreads his arms as he walks toward me, saying, "There is one thing I will not tolerate in my classroom and that is students who are not serious about being here. Miss Hill, please gather your things and leave."

What the hell? The man looks like Santa Claus, but he's Satan. I glance at Carter, but the ass turns away with a smile on his face. "I *am* serious about this class, sir."

"Then prove it, Miss Hill."

The other students won't look at me now. I'm a freaking pariah. Why is he doing this to me? I'm a serious artist, but this has happened before. The other people see my young face and try to throw me out. Screw that. I'm not leaving. Folding my arms over my chest, I lean back in my seat. "I belong here as much as anyone else in this class. Just because I missed a day—"

"Exactly. You missed a day. You failed to notify me, didn't bother to prepare for today's lesson, and you had to bum a syllabus off of the gentleman sitting next to you. All of those things combined tell me that you're not serious and I don't have time to play art class, Miss Hill. We're serious people and you've proven that you are not, unless...?"

Carter flicks his eyes my way and gives an almost imperceptible shake of his head, but I'm already speaking. "Unless what?"

"Unless you want to prove to the class, and myself, that you are, in fact, a serious artist and won't waste anymore of our precious time." Evil Santa stares me down, but I don't look away.

My jaw is set, locked, to keep from cursing him out. What an assface. "Fine. Done."

The professor smirks. "You aren't going to ask what I mean by that?"

"No. I'm all in, as long as it's art and you didn't just sucker me into washing your car for the semester." I glare at him, hoping I earned a little respect. The man seemed so nice when he first walked in the room. It's weird that he did a one-eighty so quickly.

"Very well. You may stay." Evil Santa continues the lesson and forgets about me.

Carter doesn't speak, but his eyes keep wandering in my direction. At the end of the class, he gathers up his books and follows me outside. Running to catch up, he falls in step beside me. "He played you, you know. You walked right into his trap." He laughs softly, but I have no idea what he's talking about.

I shrug. "What's he going to have me do? Clean the desks and knead all the erasers until my hands cramp?"

The corners of Carter's lips twitch as he tries to hide his amusement. "Nope. You just signed up to be the model in the Tuesday night figure drawing class."

"What?" I stop walking and every thought flies out of my head. "I did not!"

He's laughing. "You totally did. He suckered you into it. Dr. Jax always pulls shit like that."

I punch Carter's arm to make him stop sniggering, but he just laughs harder. "I can't be a model!"

"No one wants to be the model. Like, ever. But it is difficult to learn how to draw when there aren't any volunteers."

I'm standing in the quad with my jaw on the grass. "I volunteered to be a model?"

"Yup."

"In a figure drawing class?"

"Yup. Now, connect the dots, freshman."

Carter's eyes sparkle, the smile on his lips growing broader.

Horrified, I look him in the face. "It's a figure drawing class, so the model is… Oh God."

Carter chuckles. "Yeah, God can't help you. You signed up to be the nude model. It'll be way better than drawing the same old, wrinkled dude that usually shows up."

My eyes shift slowly to the side, and glance at him. "You're in that class?"

"Kerry, every upper classmen in the department is in that class. Don't worry. I bet you won't be the only model he suckers into it."

"Really?" I ask hopefully.

"No. I seriously doubt it. I was just trying to make you feel better." He pauses and smiles. "Come on, it's not like it matters. You've drawn nudes before." Carter tugs my elbow and starts us walking toward the main building.

My feet move slowly, but my mind is reeling, spinning like a top, struggling to figure out how to get out of this situation. "Yeah, I've drawn nudes, but they're other people. I'm not a model! Carter, you have to help me."

"I tried." I give him a look and he amends his statement. "Okay, I didn't try very hard. I'm selfish and you're beautiful. I bet he lets you wear a drape or something. Don't worry about it."

"I'm going to puke."

Carter pulls the glass doors open and walks inside with me. We grab lunch and he takes me over to a table filled with art freaks. My people. I sit down next to a guy with blue hair and a pierced face, like everything is pierced—his nose, eyebrow, cheek, lip, and tongue.

Blue-haired boy points a fork at me. "Who's the new girl?"

Carter answers, "Kerry Hill. She fell for Jax's setup."

Blue looks me over and shrugs. "Score."

I want to bury my face in my mashed potatoes and die. "Why doesn't the school hire models? Like, real models who don't care about taking off their clothes in public?"

Sitting across from me, a girl wearing a solid black outfit laughs, "Like that'll ever happen. They're tightwads and don't want to pay for it. So we get to draw the same old geezer over and over. Frankly, it'll be nice not drawing wrinkles for a change." She glances up at me and points her fork at my chest. "Don't you dare back out of it."

Carter answers, before I can explain. "She can't. Kerry made a public declaration that she was up for whatever he could dish out."

Goth Girl's eyes widen slightly. "You poor kid. He really suckered her that badly?" Carter nods. "What an asswipe. Did he ask you to leave?" I nod. "Yeah, he did the same thing to me a couple of years ago."

"You modeled?"

She laughs, like I'm adorable. "Hell no. He needed a sucker to rebuild the class parade float in two nights because some asshole got shitfaced and torched it to the ground." She stuffs a piece of hotdog into her mouth and adds, "It sucked."

Carter looks over at me. "It won't be that bad."

"Yeah, for you," I say tightly. My world is spinning so fast, my body feels like it's on the Gravitron at the county fair.

Carter's face turns red with embarrassment and he looks away. Oh, my

God. This is not happening. To make matters worse, Josh chooses this moment to join the conversation. "Hey, Kerry! How'd your conquest go? Did you nail him?" Josh puts his hand on my shoulder before sitting down next to me.

Goth Girl snorts, watching the embarrassment visibly spreading across my face, like fire on a dried out Christmas tree. "Fuck it." I toss down my silverware.

"That's what he said," Josh jokes, before putting his hand over mine. "Come on, there's no way it was that bad."

Carter's eyes are on the side of my face, reassessing what he thinks of me based on this new information. No wonder Beth wants to kill her brothers. I elbow Josh in the ribs and try to stand up.

"Rebound guy," I explain to the table of strangers. Oh, my God! I want to drag Josh outside and let the oddly large collection of campus cats eat his face off. "This one told me it's the fastest way to mend a broken heart." I jab my thumb at him.

"No one thinks you're a slut, Kerry." Josh offers. "That'd be shallow. They don't even know you."

What the hell is he doing? "No, they don't—at least they didn't. So, thanks for sharing my messed up love life with a group of strangers. Appreciate it." My tone is getting sharper and sharper, because the wounds are still too new. It might be funny in a month, or a year, but not right now.

Goth Girl kicks Josh under the table. "Stop being a dick, Josh."

Josh makes a face. "I am not a dick, Emily. She didn't know any of you—well, except for him, and let's face it, he's Carter—there's not much to know." Carter presses his lips together like he wants to kill Josh, but he doesn't say anything. "Now you guys like her and it's all because of me." He smiles his flashy, pretty-boy grin, and jumps up. "Catch you later, surrogate little sister."

When he leaves, I slam my head on the table. "Oh shit, he adopted me."

"He likes you," Carter says tightly.

Emily taps the table in front of Carter. "No, he doesn't. He's doing the same shit to her that he does to his little sister, Beth." Emily makes a face at him and then chugs her container of milk.

Carter scowls at her and I realize there's

more story here that I don't know. Lifting my face a little more, I ask, "You guys know him?"

No one answers. Finally, Emily rolls her eyes and huffs. "Yeah, we know him. Carter and Josh used to be best friends."

"What happened?" I ask. Normally, I wouldn't have, but they all know a crapload of stuff about me and I still know very little about them.

"We're not friends anymore." Carter gets up without looking at me, collects his food and walks off.

The table is too quiet and I just lost my only connection to this group of people. An uneasy swirling in my stomach leads me to say, "I'm sorry. I didn't mean to—"

Emily offers a half smile. "It's not you. Josh stole Carter's girlfriend. They cheated for a while without telling him. It wasn't pretty when Carter found out. No one talks about it, so whenever Josh is around, that's the elephant in the room no one will acknowledge. So, New Girl, what's your next class?"

"Uh, Art History III." The table looks at me weird, so I shrug. "I'm kind of an art nerd."

CHAPTER 7

Walking to the grocery store is getting old. I took the bus to the mall. It was an adventure I have no desire to repeat any time soon. The driver seemed to have stepped directly out of a zombie flick. We're lucky we didn't all die on the way over here. Now, I'm stranded at the mall, camped out in a little café with my laptop, scouring Craigslist for a cheap car.

"Hey Kerry!" I look up to see Beth across the hallway, waving at me. I smirk and wave back. She runs over and takes the seat across from me. Beth has a lot more money than I do and the shopping bags to prove it. "What are you doing?"

"Shopping for a car."

"You don't need a car." I glance up at her and give her an expression that says she's nuts. "I meant, you don't need your own car. You can borrow my stylish soccer mom car whenever you want."

I'm touched; I really am, especially since she has a nice new car. But I can't be a leech like that. "Thanks, Beth, but I think I need my own set of wheels. I need a job." I at least need a temporary job—and before next Tuesday night, so I don't have to be the damned figure-drawing model. How stupid am I? I didn't think professors did things like that to students, but what do I know?

"Oh," she scoots around and looks over the screen with me. "What about that one?"

"It's too much money. It has to be under a thousand."

Beth gives me a smile. "It is under a hundred thousand."

"Ha, ha, very funny." I look up and can tell from the look on Beth's face she isn't joking. "I meant under a grand. I only have a couple thousand bucks in the bank and it has to last me until the end of the semester."

Beth's eyes nearly bug out of her head.

"Are you serious?" I nod. "Your parents aren't going to send you more money?"

A bitter laugh jumps out before I can stop it. "Uh, no. They're not like that. It's okay, Beth. I can handle this as long as I can find something that runs. This one looks good. It just popped up." The ad says it's for an old VW Bus. I smile at the screen. I've always thought those were cool in a hippie sort of way. I could paint big flowers on the sides and get a fuzzy steering wheel cover.

Beth nods slowly. "It gets good gas mileage, too. Well, good for a van." I give her a strange look, not expecting a rich girl to know crap about cars. "I know stuff," she says, offended.

Smiling at her, I nod. "I see that. Do you know how to change a flat?"

She offers a sharp smile and nods. "Do you know how to change the oil?"

"Touché," I laugh. "I won't make rich girl assumptions anymore."

"I'm not rich." Beth is leaning in close to the computer screen when she says it, trying to read the listing.

"Where are your glasses?" It's just a hunch, but I've noticed she holds everything up to her nose to read, so it's kind of obvious by now.

She backs up and smiles sheepishly at me. "In my room."

"Why aren't they on your face?"

"Oh, God, you sound like my mother. They're stupid, that's why. I can't wear contacts and the glasses are Coke bottles. I look like a lunatic with them on."

"You look kind of crazy trying to make out with my laptop. The glasses can't be that bad." She sneers at me. "Oh, come on."

"Fine, if you can actually look at them and tell me that with a straight face, I'll wear them."

She's made this bet before. I can tell from her smug expression and tiny smile. "Deal, and you're wearing them when you're driving."

"I don't need them for driving."

"How do you read the signs?"

She laughs. "Yeah, I don't read signs." No kidding. This explains her mad driving skills. I bet she can barely see the lines on the road.

"I noticed." I glance at her, and send the guy who owns the van a message. Beth and I chat for a few more moments. While we chat, the van owner responds with a list of recent repairs, including new tires and a new starter. There's a picture of it in a grassy lot, flanked by several other vehicles. It looks rust-free. Score. "I'm going to call him. Will you drive me to pick it up, if I buy it?"

"Psh, like you have to ask?" She leans in close to the screen while I walk away with the phone next to my ear.

It rings forever and someone finally picks up. "Hello?" A guy says in broken English.

"Hi. I just messaged you about the VW Bus. Listen, I know you were asking $1500, but is there any way you'll wiggle on the price?" My heart is racing. I want this van. I can already picture myself in it. I'm going to get little pink curtains for the back windows. It's going to be bitchin'!

"Wag gul?" he asks like he doesn't understand.

"Yes, will you take $1000? That's all I have."

"You no do $1500?"

"No, I can't. I only have one thousand."

"I do PayPal for that price. You pick up today?"

I try not to squeal. "Yes. Sounds great."

"Ok. I send you invoice. You pay and pick up by 5. Bus is yours. I no sell to no one else."

I hang up and skip back to the table, completely and totally excited. This is the best thing that's happened to me since I came down here.

CHAPTER 8

This is the worst thing that's happened to me since I came down here. WTF? He can't be serious. I circle the vehicle I bought with Beth gaping behind me. My arms are folded across my chest and I'm ready to have an aneurism. I point at the thing in front of me, and repeat, "I did not buy this. I bought that." I point to the VW Bus parked on the grass next to it.

The little Asian man shakes his head and points at the papers from PayPal. "No, you buy bus. This is bus. Right here." He slaps the sides of the vehicle and nods way too much. Yes, it's a bus all right. Apparently, I bought a bus. No, not a VW bus, but an actual little yellow school bus that's three decades old, burnt out on the inside, and with a generous heaping of rust on the outside.

"No, I bought that! I called. I said I wanted it, and you said you'd take a thousand bucks for it." I'm whine-yelling at the man, but he still smiles at me.

"Yes, you buy bus." He pats the yellow beast again and gives me a thumbs up.

"No, not that one. That one." I gesture toward the van and point excessively, jabbing the air with my finger. "I bought that one."

His dark eyes are kind and he just stands there smiling. "You buy bus. Nice bus. Run good."

I slap my palms to my face and try not to scream. Seriously. I've been at this forever and I'm not getting anywhere. I turn to Beth and say, "Please help."

She steps daintily through the gravel and mud towards us, holding up the hem of her trademark hippie skirt. "Uh, sir, Mr. Nice Man, she wants that one." Beth walks over to him and then actually crosses to the van and taps it. "This one."

I glance at the guy, hopeful that he understands, and he does because his smile widens. "You want van?"

"Yes!"

He nods and says, "Fifteen hundred dollar."

My face falls. "But you said I could have it for a thousand."

"No, bus cheaper. Van fifteen hundred dollar." He leans forward, nodding over and over again. The man is shorter than me and if I had the slightest inclination that he was screwing with me, I'd run him over with his yellow bus. The thing is, I don't think he is. He's been smiling and nodding at other people, and several of the girls in my hallway said he's a great guy with cheap cars. No one mentioned a goddamn bus.

I groan and look over at Beth, before telling the guy, "I guess I need to cancel my payment. I don't want a bus."

"Yes, you buy bus. It nice." He pats the side again.

"No, I didn't want that." I point at the thing and shake my head. "I need to cancel the transaction."

"No cancel. Bus. You want bus, bus is here. Bus!"

"Beth, kill me. Please."

She tries again. "She doesn't want that one. She wants the other one."

"Yes, extra money."

"No!" I yell and my tiny voice suddenly sounds very loud as it travels through the yard. The few other people looking at old cars look my way. "No extra money."

The man shakes his head and looks at Beth and then back at me. "What she want?" Beth points to the van and he lights up again. "Fifteen hundred dollar."

"Uh," Beth interjects, "why don't I just spot you the difference. You can pay me back."

"Because I don't have an extra $500, and I'll never pay you back."

She shrugs and looks at the ground. Following her gaze, I notice that her pretty Chinese slippers are covered in mud. "I know that," she says. "I was being nice."

It must be nice to have money and kick it around like it doesn't matter, but I'm not a leech. "Thanks, but no. I have to do this on my own."

"You realize what you're saying, right?"

Looking up at the yellow bus, I nod. "Fuck, yeah. I'm going to be the girl who drives around in a burnt-out school bus. Score."

CHAPTER 9

I drive the bus back to the dorm and have issues finding a place to park. I head over by the lot where the school has their nice shiny new buses and park it there. No one will notice, right? As I climb down the steps, a guy in a uniform comes over. "You can't park that here."

"Why not? It's a school bus." He gives me a look that says to get the bus off his lot. "Fine."

I march back up the stairs and drive it back around campus to my dorm. I bet they make me buy three parking permits because that's how many parking slots I need. After waiting for well over two hours, three slots open up and I manage to pull the thing in.

Just as I pull the key out of the ignition, I hear a noise. It sounds weird, and it's not a mechanical machine sound. It's more like a nail on metal. I walk past the rows of seats and the disgustingly dirty windows. There is so much trash in back that it's revolting.

My foot connects with an old Coke can and sends it skittering to the back of the van. It collides with the wall and something stirs. The hairs on my arms prickle just before the wild screech hits my ears and a seriously pissed off raccoon jumps up from the pile of junk on the floor. It claws up to the top of the seatback and hisses at me, its body in a pissed off cat stance, complete with arched back.

Screaming like a lunatic, I run away, leaving the keys in the ignition, and sprint straight up the stairs into the dorm. When I make it to the third floor, I fall out of the stairwell and gasp at the window, looking down at my bus below.

I'm close to crying. I spent all my money on a rotten bus with a rabid raccoon in the back. My bottom lip is quivering when Emily steps up next to me. She leans in before I realize she's there and says, "What are we looking at?" I scream at the top of my lungs and she screams back as my heart explodes, and then she adds, "Well, that was fun. What the hell is wrong with you?" She's laughing at me and looking out the window.

Clutching my heart, I stutter, "Don't do that!"

Emily plays with the leather strap around her neck and rolls her eyes. I can't tell if she likes me or if she thinks I'm mental. "You look a little freaked."

"I am!" It all gushes out before I can stop. "Nothing is going the way it should be! It's not just the modeling thing, it's everything! My boyfriend dumped me, Josh told you guys I'm a whore, my roommate is a bitch, a really hot guy walked out on me last night, and to top things off I bought a bus with a fucking raccoon in the back." I try to shut up and mash my lips together, but they quiver. "I didn't know he was back there. I kicked a can and it must have hit him, because he jumped at me with his little paws and…" I'm holding up my hands up like they're paws and a smile cracks across my face because I look ridiculous and it sounds really funny.

Well, it would be if it happened to someone else. I laugh once, and drop my hands and look out the window. "See that piece of shit?"

Emily steps toward the window. "Yeah. It's kinda hard not to."

"That's mine."

"Bitchin'. And I like how you took up three prime parking spots with your inconspicuous, rodent infested vehicle." Emily gives me a crooked smile and we both look out at the bus.

"No one will notice."

"No, of course not." She's trying so hard not to laugh, which makes me like her even more. Turning toward me, she adds, "I have heard some very shitty first week of college stories, but yours is the worst. You win. Hands down."

I smile primly and bow at the waist. "Thank you. Thank you so much. I'd like to thank my mother for sending me here with no money, and my father for only paying my tuition. Lastly, I'd like to thank the naked man who was lovely to look at while it lasted."

Emily can't help it, she starts laughing and I laugh with her, because it's either that or cry. "You crack me up. Like, seriously."

"If anything, my life is amusing."

"So, what kind of gas mileage does that thing get?"

"I don't know, but it's pretty bad. Like a mile a gallon. That beast is personally responsible for the hole in the ozone layer."

Emily laughs again, and then pulls her long dark hair back into a ponytail. It's jet black, but I think she dyed it because her eyebrows are so light, blonde almost. "A bunch of us are going out later. Do you want to come?"

"Where are you going?"

"Does it matter?"

"No." I pause, and after a second add, "Hey, you're not just asking me because you need a bus driver, are you?"

"I call dibs on the seat next to the rodent."

"You can have the rodent."

"I might take you up on that."

After figuring out where I'm supposed to meet up with Emily later, I head to my room. I need to change and unwind before I lose my mind. Lucky me. Roommate is in there. "Hey," I offer before I flop down on my bed, face first into a pillow.

"You have a package downstairs." She points a manicured nail toward the desk we share. There's a UPS call slip.

I wonder why they didn't bring the boxes up, but don't ask. Roommate is being nice and I don't want to spoil it. Pushing off the bed, I cross the room and grab the slip. I don't want to walk downstairs, but I want my clothes. That's what's in the boxes. I shipped them because I didn't have time to pack up my room before I left. I didn't plan on coming to college here and it was a three-day drive. By the time I decided to come, there wasn't enough time, so my parents threw my clothes in boxes and shipped them the cheapest way possible. I've been living out of a suitcase for the past week.

After walking down the stairs, I go to the girl at the desk and ask where my boxes are. "Let me see your paper." I hand her the call tag. She snaps her gum and points out the doors. "This is going to be in the student center by the mailboxes. Go to the window and ask them."

Damn it. I don't want to walk across campus and get them. There are seven boxes and I bet each one is heavier than I am.

Taking the slip back, I thank her and start my walk across campus. By the time I get to the mail window, it's about to close.

"Wait!" I yell and run the last few steps. The woman in the window looks like she's going to shut it anyway, so I lunge the call slip at her and slap it down on the counter. "I need these."

She picks up the slip and looks it over before disappearing into the back. As I wait, I glance around at the other students. They all seem like they have friends and that they know what's going on. No one looks lost or like they feel the way I do. It's nearly dinnertime. I see Carter push through the doors with a bunch of other guys that I haven't seen before. I nod my head at him, wondering if he's going to blow me off or say hello. To my surprise, he walks away from the man pack and heads my way. "Hey, Kerry."

"Hey, yourself. My boxes finally got here." I rub my palms together and smile at him.

"Boxes?"

"Yeah, my cheap-o parents mailed all my stuff after they threw my butt on a plane. I'm lucky they didn't buy me a seat on the livestock flight."

He smirks. "I'm sure." He pushes his hands into the pockets of his jeans that are two sizes too big.

The woman returns with a blank look on her face and no boxes. "Honey, you need to call the number on this slip." She shoves it at me and reaches over her head to close the window.

"Wait, why? Where are my things?"

"From the looks of it, this entire lot was shipped to Guam."

"What?"

She says it louder, like I didn't hear. "Guam." And then she pulls the metal screen down and disappears from sight. I'm still staring blankly at the closed window when Carter reaches in front of me and picks up the paper.

"Come and have dinner. We can get your boxes back. I can even call if you want. It's not a big deal, Kerry."

"You're just saying that." I smile a tiny bit and look over at him.

"Yeah, but it made you smile. Come on."

Carter is on the phone for a long time and I don't say much. Emily interjects that I got a new car, but stops talking when I slam my heel down on her toe under the table. She didn't really feel it, thanks to those military boots she's always wearing. Tonight she has on a studded black collar, a tight black top layered with a leather jacket, and a pleated blue and black skirt with rocker stockings—the kind that look like a cat clawed them before they were sent to the store and put on the shelf.

"So, where are we going?" I ask, changing the subject before they hear about my bus. My plan is to deny ownership and hope to God that someone is stupid enough to steal it. Or that the raccoon starts a fire, because he looked a little crazy if you ask me. Those tiny paws could pull off arson. Maybe I should throw some matches in the back later.

"There's a club in the city that's really cool. It's like a club, a coffee house, a poetry reading, and an art show all in one place." The guy speaking is named Noah. He's barely said two words to me before now. He's rail thin and tall, with a mop of sandy blonde hair and a nose that's too big for his face. "It's cool. You'll like it."

Carter hangs up and looks over at me.

"So, I, uh, have some news." He says it carefully, like he expects me to have a public meltdown. "Your boxes—all seven of them—are, in fact, in Guam."

"Why? They were supposed to come here. How'd they end up there?"

"Well, that's the funny thing about it. No one seems to know, but they did find your stuff." He hesitates, like he doesn't want to tell me.

"And?" I prompt.

"And your stuff is at an orphanage. They, uh, thought it was a donation and opened the boxes, but UPS said your things will be boxed back up and rerouted, wait—Kerry…" I'm up and walking away from the table. I have to move or I'm going to lose it. He catches up with me as I push through the doors and head outside into the night air.

"Thanks for trying, Carter. I appreciate it."

"They can get you your stuff back. It's not lost, Kerry." He touches my elbow and stops, so I turn to face him.

I shake my head. "I can't ask people who have less than me to send it back, never mind homeless, motherless, children." My mind is spinning because I know what the decision means. I'll be wearing the same three outfits for the next sixteen weeks.

"So, what are you going to do?"

"I don't know. Buy a butt load of gym clothes and wear those." If you wanted a formula for being the most unpopular, weirdest kid on campus, that's it: gym clothes girl. Like I need another reason for my roommate to call me Bacon.

"Seriously?" He can't tell if I'm kidding around or not.

I glance up at him. "Yeah, I'm not loaded like most of the kids here, but I can get by." I start to walk again, and wrap my arms around my middle. I feel lost, like I'm floating. There are too many problems and not enough ways to fix them. When I notice Carter isn't beside me, I look back. He's standing there with his lips parted, staring. "What?"

"Nothing. You just surprise me. I've never met someone like you."

"Me neither, and it's nothing worth noting."

Carter walks up to me and says, "Yes it is. You gave away all your earthly possessions without a second thought. Who does that?"

"Uh, people who have their earthly possessions accidentally shipped to Guam? Seriously, it wasn't voluntary so you can't be impressed."

He gives me a lopsided smile. "You don't give yourself enough credit."

"It's not like I did it on purpose, Carter, so don't act like I did. If I had things my way, I would have my boxes. The Universe is out to get me, so I don't fight back anymore. That's all it is. I'm lazy."

"I doubt that." He looks me over once and asks, "Did you really just break up with someone?"

I don't want to look at him, but I manage to answer. "That was very PC, but yeah, he dumped me."

"His loss, Kerry. Seriously. The guy's an idiot." I look up at him and see a faint smile. "So, are you still coming with us?"

"I don't know. I don't really feel like it and I have nothing to wear."

"Screw that shit, Freshman." Emily is there again, racing up behind us. "We're about the same size and I have a dress you can use. It'll be awesome. Come on." She takes my hand and tugs me back to the dorm.

CHAPTER 10

Two hours later, I'm dressed like someone else, again, and wandering around a club in Austin. I'm wearing a short leather skirt, a pair of combat boots and a thin top that is way too short. If I raise my hands, the bottom of my bra sticks out. It barely covers my boobs. All around me, live music is blaring. Emily and the other people I came with are all dancing like head bangers. I wander off on my own to look at paintings they've already seen a million times.

The hairs on my arms prickle when I feel eyes on me. I glance around, but don't see who's looking. Smoothing my skin, I step around the painting to the other side, and gaze at it. I like this one. It's cool blues, blacks, and purples mixing together like soul sucking shadows. They almost seem alive.

"I thought I saw you." His voice drifts lazily over my shoulder and I stiffen. Mystery Man steps to the side and tries to catch my eye. He doesn't say why he ran out on me and I don't ask. I won't look at his face, because if I see those eyes I know I'll melt and I'm not letting this guy humiliate me for a third time.

"Yeah, you did." I clutch my drink like it's a lifeline and chant to myself over and over again, *just look at the painting, just look at the painting.*

"Do you like this piece?"

"Does it matter?" My tone says, 'fuck off.'

He looks a little shocked and then surprises me. "Yes, because it's mine."

I turn and look at him. "You're a horrible liar."

"No, I'm serious." He steps forward and points to the little gold plaque next to the painting. Nathan Smith. "That's me."

"Sure, Smitty."

"You don't believe me?" He looks shocked and there's a big beautiful smile on his face that says as much.

"No."

He smiles and works his jaw, before reaching into his pocket. I wish he'd leave, but he doesn't. He stands there with me, a step too close. "Here." He hands me his ID. NATHAN SMITH. Damn, even his driver's license picture looks perfect. Mine looks like aliens were chewing on my toes.

I hand it back to him. "Lovely."

"You aren't going to give me a second chance, are you?"

Turning, I smile up at him. "Not a chance in Hell." I walk to the next piece and fold my arms over my chest as I look it over.

Nathan is trailing me and smiling that cocky grin that guys wear when a woman shoots them down. He mirrors my pose, which makes his arms look lickable. "Exactly what part of Hell has to freeze over before you give me another try? The foyer? The basement?"

I don't want to laugh, but the idea of Hell having a basement is funny. I get a picture in my head of an old guy burying bodies at the bottom of a staircase, next to a creepy furnace. It amuses me. "Level nine, ya know, the basement."

He presses his hand to his heart. "That's a long ways down."

"Yes, but the fall was fast. I bet you hit your ass on the way down." I turn and look at his backside and then up into his face. Damn, he's hot. I remember the way that body looked naked and try to push the memories away.

"Nice," he grins and I realize that I'm flirting with him. I remember what Beth's brother said and try to walk away, but he follows me to the next painting. "I could say something inappropriate about your ass, but I think that'll only bury me further."

I laugh and look over my shoulder at him. "You are never seeing this ass again, or any other part of me, so walk away. You're good at that."

"Ouch." He grins harder. "You realize what you just did, don't you?"

"Yeah, I told you to go to Hell and leave me alone."

Nathan steps into my space and looks down into my eyes. As the music pounds through my body, his scent fills my head. "That's not what your eyes say. Or your lips."

He lifts his hand and touches the center of my lower lip lightly.

I can't move. He's so beautiful and my body responds to him so quickly. My heart thumps wildly as I tear my eyes away. "Yeah, well, then you need a hearing aid, old man. You might want to get your vision checked, too, because I think you're a little bit on the blind side." I scratch my temple, overtly using only my middle finger.

He doesn't comment. Nathan continues to beam at me and ignores my crude gesture. "Only because of your radiant beauty."

"Oh, my God! You did not just use that line on me."

"I think I did." He steps so close to me that his chest brushes mine. A jolt of electricity shoots through my body. Bastard.

I don't move, but I should. We're way too close. "What's the matter? Didn't have a drawing of me to whip out this time?"

He leans in kissably close and whispers, "I could whip out something else I know you like."

I flinch like he slapped me and growl, "Fuck you."

"Anytime." He gives me that boyish

smirk and I want to rip it off his beautiful face.

"I wasn't offering."

"You don't have to. I can tell that you want me."

"Yeah, I want you about as much as I want hemorrhoids. Walk away, pretty boy. I'm not changing my mind."

"You will." He winks at me and turns on his heel. I watch him walk away, even though I don't want to. When I look up, I see Carter watching me. I smile at him and then follow his gaze across the room to Nathan with a sinking feeling inside my stomach.

Oh, God. They know each other.

SECRETS & LIES, VOL. 2

To ensure you don't miss the next installment, text AWESOMEBOOKS (one word) to 22828 and you will get an email reminder on release day.

*****

Coming Soon

BROKEN PROMISES
A Trystan Scott Novel

More Ferro Family Books

NICK FERRO
~THE WEDDING CONTRACT~
*****

BRYAN FERRO
~THE PROPOSITION~
*****

SEAN FERRO
~THE ARRANGEMENT~
******

PETER FERRO GRANZ
~DAMAGED~
******

JONATHAN FERRO
~STRIPPED~
******

TRYSTAN SCOTT
~COLLIDE~
******

More Romance Books by H.M. Ward

DAMAGED

DAMAGED 2

STRIPPED

SCANDALOUS

SCANDALOUS 2

SECRETS

THE SECRET LIFE OF TRYSTAN SCOTT

And more.

To see a full book list, please visit:
www.SexyAwesomeBooks.com/books.htm

Can't Wait for H.M. Ward's Next Steamy Book?

★★★★★

Let her know by leaving stars and telling her what you liked about
Secrets & Lies
in a review!

Made in the USA
San Bernardino, CA
06 August 2014